Howie Monroe and the Doghouse of Doom

Tales from the House of Bunnicula Books by James Howe

It Came from Beneath the Bed!
Invasion of the Mind Swappers from Asteroid 6!
Howie Monroe and the Doghouse of Doom

Other Bunnicula Books by James Howe:

Bunnicula (with Deborah Howe)
Howliday Inn
The Celery Stalks at Midnight
Nighty-Nightmare
Return to Howliday Inn
Bunnicula Strikes Again!

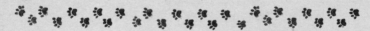

James Howe is the author of the award-winning bestseller, *Bunnicula*, and its sequels, as well as many other popular books for young readers, including *The Misfits* and the Pinky and Rex series for younger readers. He lives in Hastings-on-Hudson, New York.

TALES FROM THE HOUSE OF BUNNICULA

Howie Monroe and the Doghouse of Doom

JAMES HOWE

ILLUSTRATED BY BRETT HELQUIST

SCHOLASTIC INC.

New York Toronto London Auckland Sydney
Mexico City New Delhi Hong Kong Buenos Aires

ISBN 0-439-52482-2

12 11 10 9 8 7 6 5 4 3 2 1   3 4 5 6 7 8/0

Printed in the U.S.A.   40

First Scholastic printing, September 2003

Book design by Ann Bobco

The text of this book is set in Berkeley.

The illustrations are rendered in acrylics and oils.

To Dan Darigan,
who has the best laugh east of the Mississippi ·
—J. H.

For Mary Jane
—B. H.

HOWIE'S WRITING JOURNAL

Last night, Pete got into trouble with Mr. and Mrs. Monroe. He was supposed to write a story for school, but he didn't, and now he's getting an eff. I don't know what that is, but it must be bad, because Mr. Monroe said, "I can't believe my son - the son of an English professor - got an eff on a writing assignment!"

Pete said, "How was I supposed to write a story when I didn't have an <u>idea</u>?"

I wonder if it's like a stain. I remember the time I got into trouble for drooling on something Mr. Monroe had written. It left a stain, but it wasn't my fault. I was just happy to see him.

Pete and I don't usually agree about things. Maybe that's because he's an eleven-year-old boy and I'm a puppy, but I think it's mostly because we don't look at things the same way. This time, though, I had to agree with him. I know what it's like trying to write when you don't have an idea.

Like now. I'm supposed to be writing a

third book in my series, <u>Tales from the House of Bunnicula</u>, and I used up all my ideas on my first two.

I asked Uncle Harold what to do. Uncle Harold wrote all those books about our rabbit, Bunnicula, so he knows a thing or two about writing.

He said, "Well, Howie, the big question a writer has to ask himself is —"

"When do I get paid?"

"That wasn't what I was going to say."

"When do I get my picture on the cover of <u>Canine Quarterly</u>?"

3

"Howie," Uncle Harold said, giving me that look he gets sometimes when he thinks I'm not taking life seriously. Personally, I don't think life should be taken seriously. Except maybe when your food dish is empty, or you really, really, <u>really</u> need to go out and everybody's saying, "It's <u>your</u> turn to walk the dog!"

Anyway, what he told me is that the big question writers ask is, "What if?" Which I guess I knew already.

"You have to put yourself in the place of others, Howie," he went on. "Ask how you'd feel if what happened to someone else happened to you. Or if you could do something impossible. Like fly."

"Or stay awake for more than two hours in a row?"

"Exactly."

I don't think a book about staying awake for two hours and fifteen minutes will sell many copies. I'd better ask a different "what if."

What if . . . what if . . . what if . . .

What if I were like that kid in the book Toby's been reading to Uncle Harold and me every night? That kid has a pretty interesting life. His parents have died, see, and he lives with these really mean relatives, but then he discovers he's got special powers, and when he goes off to a school to learn how to use them, he finds out he's famous and . . .

That's it! I know just what I'm going to write!

Hey, that "what if" comes in pretty handy.

Maybe if Pete had used it, he wouldn't have gotten an eff.

Howie Monroe and the Doghouse of Doom

By Howie Monroe

CHAPTER 1:
"THE IMPORTANT LETTER"

Howie Monroe was as smart as a whip and as cute as a button, but that didn't stop him from being an orphan. He lived with his mean aunt and uncle, Mr. and Mrs. Monroe, and their wretched, runny-nosed sons, Toby and Pete.

(NOTE to the real Monroes: This is only a story! You are not mean, wretched, or runny-nosed.) (Except maybe for Pete.) (Sometimes.)

7

The Monroes made Howie sleep under Pete's bed, which was a dark and scary place, full of all kinds of creepy stuff, including several generations of dust bunnies. (See Book 1: *It Came from Beneath the Bed!* by Howie Monroe.) They were so mean to him, they fed him every other day and even then, were so stingy, they gave him only Kibbles *or* Bits.

Howie Monroe dreamed of a better life where he would not be called "dumb dog" all the time and everyone would recognize how special he was.

How, do you ask, did he know he was special? He knew because when he noticed his face reflected in his water dish, he saw that he was as cute as a button; when he did the crossword puzzle in his mind while sleeping under the single sheet of newspaper that was some-times provided for warmth on cold winter nights, he knew he was as smart as a whip; and, besides, he had a mysterious pain in his back left leg that he was sure was a mark of his being an unusual dog with special powers.

One day, he got a letter in the mail. It was a good thing that none of the Monroes were home. Otherwise, Pete and Toby would have folded it into a paper airplane and flown it over his head while he yipped and chased after it. This time, he ran quickly to read it under Pete's bed, and what a lucky thing he did because it was a letter that would change his life forever!

Dear Resident, it began promisingly, *You, too, could be a dog wizard! Take this simple test to find out!*

1. Do you live with cruel relatives who make you sleep in a dark and scary place?

Howie looked around at the cobwebs and dust bunnies. Check!

2. Do you have an unusual physical characteristic that has great significance that won't be revealed to you until an important point in the story?

Howie thought of the bursitis in his back left leg. Check!

3. Do you have a spirit of adventure, a sharp mind, and ten bucks to return with the enclosed application to the Dogwiz Academy for Canine Conjurers?

Howie glanced at the crumpled ten-dollar bill lying under a heap of Pete's smelly, dirty socks. Check!

Yes! He was going to the Dogwiz Academy for Canine Conjurers! He, Howie Monroe, cute, adorable, but pitiful enough to make the reader feel sorry for him, was going to find out how special he really was!

He might even get to eat Kibbles *and* Bits!

Howie's Writing Journal

Uncle Harold said I'm off to a good start, although the story reminded him of something, but he couldn't place it. Then he said he didn't think my readers would know what "bursitis" is. When he asked me how I knew what it was, I told him I'd heard Mr. Monroe complaining about his bursitis after attempting a full lotus position while doing one of his yoga tapes. Uncle Harold felt I should define "bursitis" for my readers.

Okay, here goes:

bur-si-tis/n: inflammation of a bursa
bur-sa/n: a bodily pouch or sac between a tendon or a bone
ten-don/n: a tough cord or band of dense white fibrous connective tissue that unites a muscle with some other part (as a bone) and transmits the force that the muscle exerts
fi-brous/adj: containing, consisting of, or resembling fibers
fi-ber/n: a thread or a structure or object resembling a thread, as

Aargh!

<u>My</u> definition of bursitis:

bur-si-tis/n: a mysterious pain in the back left leg that has great significance that won't be revealed until an important point in the story.

CHAPTER 2:
"WIZ-ON-WHEELS"

Even though Howie was a daring, adventurous, and ready-for-anything kind of puppy, he didn't want to go to the Dogwiz Academy for Canine Conjurers all by himself, so he asked his best friend, Delilah, to go with him. He knew she would like the idea of going to school because she was very, very, very, very, very, very smart. (See Book 2: *Invasion of the*

15

Mind Swappers from Asteroid 6!™ by Howie Monroe.)

Delilah was a dog who lived down the street. She had curly blonde ears, long eye-lashes that moved faster than a humming-bird's wings, and, as was mentioned in the previous paragraph, a fine mind in good working order.

Following the directions contained in the let-ter he received after sending in his application and ten bucks, Howie led Delilah to the place where they were to wait for a minivan with the words "Wiz-on-Wheels" written on its side.

The place was an abandoned gas station on the wrong side of the tracks. When the Wiz-on-Wheels showed up, the doors would open, and they were to say, "Ippity-up."

"I'm ever so grateful you invited me to join you, Howie," Delilah said in a British accent as they waited.

"Why are you speaking in a British accent?" Howie asked.

Delilah did not have an answer for this. It was only the beginning of things-not-being-what-they-had-been-before-becoming-oddly-strangely-different.

Suddenly, a van the color of night—well, more like dusk, really—pulled up in front of the abandoned gas station on the wrong side of the tracks. The doors opened. It was impossible to see inside.

Howie and Delilah looked at each other, gulped, and said, "Ippity-up!"

All at once they were floating through the

air, up, up, up into the van. The door closed behind them.

"All aboard for Dogwiz!" said a disembodied voice. The van lurched forward. There was no driver in sight.

"Wow!" said Howie as he looked at the other dogs already seated.

"Blimey!" said Delilah.

"Hello," said the scraggly-looking puppy Howie sat down beside. Besides. Beside. Next to.

"Hello," said Howie. "Who are you?"

"I'm Snivel," said the dog. "I'm poor, but please don't hold that against me. I come from a long line of canine conjurers. My brothers and sisters all went to Dogwiz, and now I'm going too. I'm going to be your new best friend."

Howie liked Snivel right away.

"I'm . . . " he started to say, by way of intro-ducing himself. But he felt a sudden twinge of pain in his back left leg. "Ooo," he moaned, "my bursitis."

"Did you say 'bursitis'?" said Snivel. "Wow, you're Howie Monroe! My new best friend is Howie Monroe!"

How did Snivel know who he was?!

Howie glanced worriedly at Delilah.

Delilah glanced worriedly at Howie.

Howie was worried that something terrible was going to happen once they arrived at Dogwiz.

Delilah was worried that she was going to be saddled with a British accent for the rest of the story.

CHAPTER 3:
"THE-EVIL-FORCE-WHOSE-NAM-C'NOT-BE-SPOKE"

When Howie arrived at Dogwiz, everyone stared at him and muttered, "That's Howie Monroe, that's Howie Monroe." Howie thought this was strange at first, but then decided it was very nice. Everyone must have read his first two books (*It Came from Beneath the Bed!* by Howie Monroe and *Invasion of the Mind Swappers from Asteroid 6!*™ by Howie

Monroe), which turned out to be true, but it was not the reason everyone recognized him. Everyone recognized him because of his bursitis.

A giant dog named Hamlet explained it all to him.

"Yer parents, Howard 'n Heather," Hamlet told him, "wer conj'rers o' th' first ord'r. I tell yeh, laddie, they wer known fer 'n wide fer the'r conj'rin'."

Howie wondered at Hamlet's way of speaking in apostrophes.

"But ther's an evil force in th' world, boyyie-lad. So evil 'iz nam c'not be spoke. When yeh speak ov 'im y'must say, The-Evil-Force-Whose-Nam-C'not-Be-Spoke."

Cool, Howie thought.

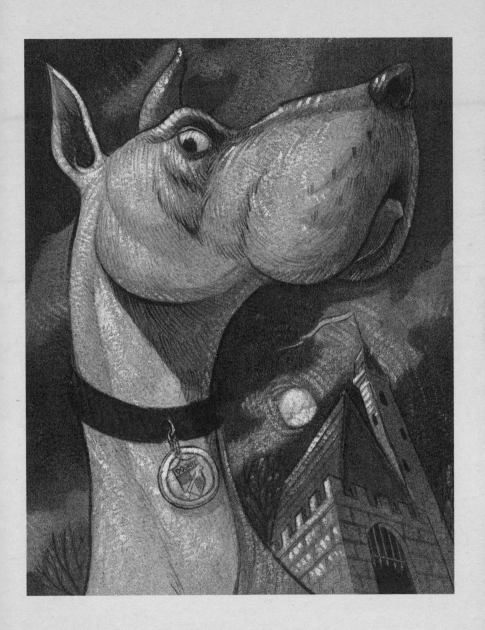

"This evil force is big," Hamlet went on.

"You mean big as in powerful?" Howie, the ever-curious dachshund puppy, asked.

"Nah, I mean big as in fat," Hamlet explained. "One day, The-Evil-Force-Whose-Nam-C'not-Be-Spoke did a tur'ble thing, the moz tur'ble thing 'e ever dun. 'E destroyed yer parents, lad, the good 'n saint'ly Howard 'n Heather—and 'e nearly destroyed U2. 'E woulda, if yeh had'n run fer it."

Howie was disturbed. How could Hamlet have used an apostrophe in "saintly" when he hadn't even dropped a letter? Still, he sensed that there were more important questions to ask.

"Why did The-Evil-Force-Whose-Nam-C'not-Be-Spoke destroy my good and saint'ly parents? How did I escape? Why don't I remember any of this? When do we get to eat?"

"Aye, yeh'll be eatin' in the Chamber o' Chow soon enuf. But before yeh go, let me tell yeh th' rest o' th' story. The-Evil-Force-Whose-Nam-C'not-Be-Spoke didn't like yer parents because o' th' way they treated 'im back in grade school. And bein' an evil force 'n all, 'e was one t' hold a grudge. 'E also did'n care fer th' way yer parents used their conj'rin' powers fer good 'n not fer evil. That jus' got on 'is nerves. So one day 'e sat on 'em."

Howie gasped. The picture that came to his mind was not a pretty one.

"They wuz squished, pure 'n simple, there's no nic'r way t' put it, boyo. But you, yeh frisky, quick-footed thing yeh, yeh ran outta the way jest in time, and all yeh were left with was—"

"Bursitis in my back left leg," Howie said, finishing the sentence for him.

"Aye," said Hamlet. "Yev got the gift, laddie-boyo-boy-kiddie-me-laddio, yer meant fer conj'rin'. That's what they'll learn ya here. But be warned: The-Evil-Force-Whose-Nam-C'not-Be-Spoke has got it in fer ya. 'E's jest been waitin' fer yeh to claim yer special powers and when yeh do . . . "

"What?" Howie asked as a cloud of concern passed over Hamlet's brow.

"Jus' don' go near the Doghouse o' Doom, that's all I ken tell ya."

The supper bell rang, and Howie, hungrier than he'd ever been in his whole life, ran off to join his friends in the Chamber of Chow. On his way, he passed a small building under a tree. The tree was whistling.

A talking frog named Hoppy said to him, "Hoppy doesn't want you to go near that small building, sir. It is not a good idea, sir."

"But why is the tree whistling?" Howie asked.

"That is the Whistling Willow," Hoppy told him. "Its music has charms and will lure you to the small building, sir, and oh, dear, sir, Hoppy cannot say the rest, sir. No, indeed, sir, it, sir, wouldn't be, sir, wise, sir."

Howie wondered why everyone spoke so oddly here, then remembered that he was the author, so he supposed it was probably because he made them talk that way.

"Is that the Doghouse of Doom?" Howie asked.

Hoppy hopped away. "Hoppy cannot say, sir. Oh, no, sir, Hoppy cannot say."

Howie stood frozen to the spot. The Whistling Willow whistled "I'm a Little Teapot," almost succeeding in luring him to the Doghouse of Doom. But the song reminded Howie that he was hungry. Off he ran to the Chamber of Chow. He could hardly wait to eat!

Howie's Writing Journal

Uncle Harold says I have an impressive vocabulary for a puppy! Wow! I impressed Uncle Harold! That means a lot to me, because I think Uncle Harold is an awesome good writer!

He told me, "I like the characters named Hamlet and Hoppy, although they seem familiar somehow."

Then he said maybe I was being a little

too self-promotional because I mentioned my other books several times. I told him I wasn't being self-promotional, I was providing valuable information to the reader.

He said, "Uh-huh," and walked away.

Well, I'd better get back to my writing. I can't wait to find out what happens next, either. Guess I'll have to write it to find out!

NOTE TO MYSELF: What does "vocabulary" mean? Look it up!

CHAPTER 4:
"BACON MALCONTENT AND THE AERIATED ELASTICUS"

That night, Howie, Delilah, and Snivel were hanging out in the student lounge, eating popcorn balls and watching *I Dream of Jeannie* on Nick-at-Nite, when Bacon Malcontent and his two stooges, Grab and Run, stepped in front of them and blocked their view.

"Excuse me," Snivel said politely, "you're blocking our view."

"Yes," said Delilah, "we're coming to one of the best bits and we'd be ever so grateful if you'd step aside."

Bacon Malcontent was a terrier whose superior breeding had left him with a permanent sneer. Grab and Run were mutts, but they'd forgotten that fact ever since Baco, as everyone called Bacon Malcontent, had let them run with him.

"So," said Baco with a sneer (which he couldn't help, since it was permanent and all), "you're the famous Howie Monroe. *Bursitis Boy.*"

Howie felt the pain in his back left leg flair up. He didn't like being called Bursitis Boy. "Yeah, so?" he replied cleverly to Baco's taunt.

"Just watch out," Baco said.

"For the Doghouse of Doom?" Howie asked.

"The Doghouse of Doom?" laughed Baco. "That's a good one, isn't it, boys?"

Grab and Run laughed too, though their eyes remained as empty as a finely tuned concert piano.

HOWIE'S WRITING JOURNAL

Uncle Howard just glanced at what I was writing and said that I used that concert piano simile in another book (see Book 1: <u>It Came from Beneath the Bed!</u> by Howie Monroe) and, besides, it doesn't make any sense.

I don't understand why things have to make sense.

Grab and Run laughed too, though their eyes remained as empty as a cat's bowl after the dog has gotten there first.

"Huh!" Baco snorted. "*Everybody* has to watch out for the Doghouse of Doom. You—*Bursitis Boy*—have to watch out for . . . *us!*"

Baco, Grab, and Run walked away, bumping into one another as they went.

Howie turned to Delilah and Snivel.

"I'm worried," Snivel said. "Baco means trouble."

Delilah immediately pulled out the notebook she carried everywhere and wrote in her glossary of magic terms: Baco = trouble.

Delilah wasn't as smart as she made you think she was.

It was in Inanimate Objects class the next

morning, while reading aloud a passage from *Flying Hydrants* by Altitudinous Airedale, that Howie found out just how much danger he was in.

A spitball hit him in the back of the head!

"Professor Sneak!" he called out. "A spitball hit me in the back of the head!"

Sneak sneered. (Howie marveled at the alliteration.)

"That is not a spitball," the professor told Howie, his words dripping contempt even as his lips dripped drool. "One would think our most . . . *gifted* . . . student would be able to recognize an Aeriated Elasticus when he is hit by one in the back of the head."

Baco, Grab, and Run snickered. Sneak snickered too.

Howie had a sudden craving for a candy bar.

"That was nothing more than a rubber band," Delilah said after class, once again proving that she *did* know a thing or two. "Someone snapped a rubber band at you, Howie, and I think I know who it was."

"Baco?"

"No."

"Grab?"

"No."

"Run?"

"No."

"Who, then?"

"It wasn't me," Snivel sniveled. "I'm your friend, Howie."

"Of course it wasn't you, Snivel," said

Delilah. She reminded herself to be patient with Snivel, who meant well, but really wasn't as smart as she was and also suffered from being a boy. "It was someone from another dimension. Someone who is determined to get you, Howie. Someone who has been after you ever since 'e flattened yer fam'ly."

Howie gasped. "Surely you don't mean—"

"Yes!" Delilah said. "I mean The-Evil-Force-Whose-Nam-C'not-Be-Spoke, whose real name, by the way, is Herbert. I read it in a book."

There was a peal of thunder. The lights dimmed and went out. It was as dark as the inside of a finely tuned concert piano. Howie wondered if the Dogwiz Academy for Canine Conjurers had forgotten to pay its electric bill.

CHAPTER 5:
"THE WRITING ON THE WALL"

When the lights came back on, Howie was all alone. A message was scrawled on the wall next to him in red paint. Or *was* it paint? Maybe . . . it . . . was . . . *ketchup!*

Howie read the words that were meant for his eyes alone:

Don't call me Herbert! My name is The-Evil-Force-Whose-Nam-C'not-Be-Spoke!

Touchy, touchy, thought Howie. But where had Delilah and Snivel gone? Howie took a step forward and slipped on a banana peel.

Someone—or some*thing*—chuckled! The message on the wall vanished! Howie thought it might be a good time to check the schedule for the next Wiz-on-Wheels out of there.

"I want to go home," he whimpered pathetically enough to make the reader reach for a tissue.

"Oh, but you can't go home, sir, no, sir, that you mustn't, sir." It was Hoppy, the talking— and increasingly annoying—frog.

"Why can't I go home?" Howie asked.

"Because you have a mission, sir," said Hoppy. "And Hoppy is here to help you achieve it. If you do, then Hoppy will be turned into his former self."

"A prince?" Howie asked.

"No, a tadpole," said Hoppy. "Hoppy was happy as a tadpole. There was so little pressure."

"There's pressure being a frog?"

"You have no idea."

It was true. Howie had no idea.

"But what is my mission?" Howie asked.

Hoppy hopped around in every direction to make sure they weren't being watched. When he was sure, he motioned for Howie to bend down. This wasn't hard, since Howie was a wirehaired dachshund and already pretty much eye to eye with the talking frog.

"You must do something Hoppy told you never to do," Hoppy told Howie.

"Talk with my mouth full?" Howie asked, surprised.

"No, that was your aunt. Hoppy told you you must never enter the Doghouse of Doom. Well, now you must, sir. You must enter the Doghouse of Doom and defeat The-Evil-Force-Whose-Nam-C'not-Be-Spoke!"

"Is that all?" the brave and daring, not to mention heroic, Howie asked.

"Actually, no," said Hoppy. "First, you must go to the Sweltering Swamp and find the lost key to the Tailwagger Triangle, where you are to go and release the Seven-Headed Schnauzer, after which you must find homes for the wandering ghosts of the Corridors of Captivity, then take a nap, following which you will crawl through the Tunnel of Terrible Things, swim the Lake of Laughable Luck, climb the Mountain of Monstrous Mischief, pass all your exams, win

44

the World Championship in Fetch for Dogwiz, and make a quarter materialize from behind Professor Sneak's right ear."

"I can do that!" Howie, the heroic and brave, not to mention daring, dachshund replied. "The nap part, anyway."

It wasn't long before Howie had gone to the Sweltering Swamp and found the key to the Tailwagger Triangle, released the Seven-Headed Schnauzer, found homes for the wandering ghosts of the Corridors of Captivity, taken a nap, crawled through the Tunnel of Terrible Things, swum the Lake of Laughable Luck, climbed the Mountain of Monstrous Mischief, taken a second nap, passed all his exams, won the World Championship in Fetch for Dogwiz, and made a quarter materialize from behind Professor Sneak's right ear.

"Piece of cake," said Howie, who wasn't even winded.

"You couldn't have done it without that second nap," Baco said, smirking. Baco smirking was even less likable than Baco sneering. "Anyway, *Bursitis Boy*, now you have to enter the Doghouse of Doom! It's been nice knowin' ya . . . *not!*"

Baco threw back his head and laughed. Grab and Run threw back their heads too, but they forgot to catch them.

In the distance, the Whistling Willow whistled "The Itsy-Bitsy Spider." Howie felt the power of the music, felt himself being pulled to the Doghouse, pulled to his fate, pulled to his . . . *DOOM?!?!?!?*"

CHAPTER 6:
"INTO THE DOGHOUSE OF DOOM"

It was the night before Howie was to face his longtime enemy, The-Evil-Force-Whose-Nam-C'not-Be-Spoke (aka Herbert), and his bursitis was hurting so badly, he could barely walk. But walk he did, all the way to the little cabin on the other side of the Sweltering Swamp, where Hamlet lived with his pet bloatfish Wanda. Delilah and Snivel went with him, mainly because Howie didn't want Delilah to be mad at him because she had such a small part in this book.

"I w'n y' t' t'k th's g'f w' y', H'wie," Hamlet told Howie as he and his friends drank the crabgrass tea Hamlet had made for them.

"Fewer apostrophes, please," the gracious and polite, not to mention well-mannered, Howie said. "I can't understand a thing you're saying."

"Sor'y," said Hamlet. "What I said was, I want yeh t' take this gift wi' yeh, Howie. It'll protect yeh from, well, from yeh know who." Hamlet handed Howie a small mirror.

Howie checked to see if he had any crabgrass stains on his teeth, then asked, "How will this protect me?"

"It is said," said Hamlet, "that the face of The-Evil-Force-Whose-Nam-C'not-Be-Spoke is so fearful, no one may look upon it without turnin' t' plastic. Ef yeh hold th' mirror afore yeh, then per'aps The-Evil-Force-Whose-Nam-C'not-Be-Spoke will see 'is own face f'rst and 'e will be turned t' plastic afore—"

"Afore *I* am turned to plastic," Howie said, finishing the sentence for him. He hated the idea of being turned to plastic. It was so permanent. Not to mention tacky. "Thank you," he said to Hamlet.

"Aye, laddie-boy-boy-lad-laddio," said Hamlet. "And don't ferget, we'll be right there wi' yeh when yeh go in t'morrow."

"Aye," said Snivel. "Tha' we will."

Delilah didn't say a word. She sniffed softly

and wiped the corner of an eye with one of her long, blonde, curly ears. A lump formed in Howie's throat. What if he went into the Doghouse of Doom and never came out? Would he ever again return to Centerville, to the family who made him miserable, but, hey, isn't that what a family's for? Would he ever again sleep under Pete's bed? Would he ever again eat Kibbles or Bits while the rest of his family gorged themselves on nine-course meals and three-layer cakes? Would he ever again get to use the words "ever again" in a sentence?

These thoughts continued to trouble him the next day as he tried to concentrate on his studies and ignore the jeers of Baco and Grab and Run. Every hour he went to the Talking

Clock to find out when he was supposed to enter the Doghouse of Doom.

"Don't fret, not yet," the Talking Clock said to him each time he approached.

But then, after leaving his Making Humans Sit, Shake, and Heel class, he heard the Talking Clock call his name: "Howie Monroe, It's Time to Go! Howie Monroe, It's Time to Go!"

Running out into the courtyard, he looked up at the face of the clock and pleaded, "Not yet! It's too soon!"

"Too soon, too late, it is your fate, at twenty past four, to go through the door."

It was now four-nineteen.

A minute later, everyone from the Dogwiz Academy for Canine Conjurers had gathered to see Howie off. Some held up signs that read,

"Good luck, Howie!" and, "We believe in you!" Howie noticed that Baco's sign read, "So long, sucka!", but what could you expect?

"I'm going in," Howie announced. Of course, with the mirror Hamlet had given him clenched between his teeth, it came out, "Ah oh-ee ih."

Ageless Duffelbag, the headmaster of Dogwiz, rushed up to Howie, tying the mirror around his neck with a ribbon so Howie wouldn't have to speak with his mouth full and confuse the reader. It was bad enough with Hamlet and all those apostrophes.

"If all else fails," Duffelbag said to Howie, "there is a spell that will turn The-Evil-Force-Whose-Nam-C'not-Be-Spoke into a bowl of split pea soup. It is—"

But before Duffelbag could say another

word, the Talking Clock boomed, "It's twenty past four, Duffelbag's a bore, the time is here, to face your fear!"

The Whistling Willow began to whistle "If You're Happy and You Know It, Clap Your Hands." Howie could not resist its siren call. He entered the Doghouse, wondering how in the world he would defeat The-Evil-Force-Whose-Nam-C'not-Be-Spoke. After all, he was only one small dachshund in a world gone mad, one tiny voice in a sea of voices, one pebble in a field of boulders, one itsy-bitsy minnow in a school of sharks!

"Hello?" he called out.

"Hello, yourself," a voice replied.

Howie's Writing Journal

That is the BEST cliff-hanger I've ever written! Now I just have to figure out who the voice belongs to. I mean, it's <u>got</u> to be The-Evil-Force-Whose-Nam-C'not-Be-Spoke, right?

Maybe not. What if there's some, like, monster waiting for Howie? Or maybe it's a ghost. Or . . .

Wait a minute. Who <u>is</u> The-Evil-Force-

Whose-Nam-C'not-Be-Spoke, anyway? I'd better figure that one out first.

This writing business involves way too much thinking.

CHAPTER 7:
"THE LAKE OF LOST ILLUSIONS"

The Doghouse was a lot bigger than it looked from the outside. Of course, Howie couldn't really tell *how* big it was because it was totally black. Black as the inside of a finely tuned . . . black as night. Still, he had the feeling it was really big because of the way his voice and the voice of whoever—or whatever—it was that answered him back echoed.

57

"Who's there . . . there . . . there?" Howie called out.

A chorus of voices answered this time. They sang, "Follow the road beneath your feet, beneath your feet, we repeat: Follow the road beneath your feet, and you will get where you're going."

No duh, thought Howie as a path lit up under his feet. With each step he took, the light continued to lead the way. Howie thought this was pretty cool, even though he didn't know where it was taking him. He figured it didn't really matter since he knew he was going to end up facing The-Evil-Force-Whose-Nam-C'not-Be-Spoke and defeating him. He would probably have to turn him into plastic, because he had the mirror and he

didn't know the spell to turn him into a bowl of split pea soup. He was disappointed. Split pea soup was his favorite. What would he do with a plastic The-Evil-Force-Whose-Nam-C'not-Be-Spoke? Wire him and turn him into a lamp, maybe.

"I heard that!" a voice boomed. It was the same voice Howie had heard when he'd first entered the Doghouse of Doom.

"Heard what?" Howie, the courageous and dauntless dachshund, replied bravely, panting just slightly enough to keep the sympathy of the reader.

"The business about the lamp," said the voice.

"You can hear my thoughts?" Howie asked.

"Just one of my many talents," said the voice. "Want to know some more?"

There was a blinding flash of light, a deafening crash of thunder, a suffocating puff of smoke, an exhausting slide show of scenes from The Evil-Force-Whose-Nam-C'not-Be-Spoke's summer vacation on the Jersey Shore . . .

"Okay, okay!" Howie cried out at last. "I get the idea!"

Suddenly, the lights went out under Howie's feet, and he found himself standing at the edge of a dimly lit lake. It was not the Lake of Laughable Luck. He'd already been there, done that. But what lake was it?

"It's the Lake of Lost Illusions," said the voice, reading Howie's thoughts.

Howie went, "Oooooo," thinking how heavy the story had suddenly become and how impressed his editor would be that he had turned literary without a moment's notice.

As Howie's eyes adjusted to the light, he made out a *thing* sitting in the middle of the lake on some kind of pod. The thing was huge. He wished he could see it better. A lamp or two wouldn't have been a bad idea.

"You've got lamps on the brain," the voice said. "But too much light is a no-no. I'm surrounded by water. If I could see my reflection, I'd turn to plastic."

"So *you're* The-Evil-Force-Whose-Nam-C'not-Be-Spoke!" Howie exclaimed.

"Gee, you're smart," said The-Evil-Force-Whose-Nam-C'not-Be-Spoke. "That must be why you get to be the hero of the story. Okay, smart guy, here you are in the Doghouse of Doom, with the entire population of the

Dogwiz Academy for Canine Conjurers and all seven of your readers just waiting for you to defeat me and prove that you're the greatest dog wizard of all time. So what're you gonna do about it, huh, huh, what're you gonna do?"

Howie wanted to think, *Gee, what an obnoxious bully—and I'll have you know I have more than seven readers, I have at least eight,* but of course he couldn't think that because the obnoxious bully would read his thoughts. Boy, he could understand why his parents didn't like this guy back in grade school.

He knew he had to think about something else instead. He thought about the mirror. This was a mistake.

"That mirror's good for nothing," said the bully on the pod. "Zero. Zip. Zilch." After running out of Z-words, he continued. "You think you're the first one to try the mirror thing? Give me a break. On second thought, I'll give *you* a break."

The ribbon around Howie's neck snapped as the mirror flew into the air and exploded into a million pieces. Or maybe thirty-seven.

"And now," said The-Evil-Force-Whose-Nam-C'not-Be-Spoke, "I'm going to do that to . . . *you!*"

Howie didn't like the sound of that. He thought of Delilah, who would miss him terribly once she'd forgiven him for giving her such a small part in this book. He thought of the Monroes, who weren't so bad once you got past their being cruel and miserable. He thought of Snivel and Hamlet and Hoppy, and

all the other new friends he'd made since coming to Dogwiz. It wasn't fair that he wouldn't get to see them again, wouldn't get to eat another meal in the Chamber of Chow, wouldn't get to write a sequel in what was destined to be the best-selling series of all time, wouldn't—

"I don't have time for so much thinking!" The-Evil-Force-Whose-Nam-C'not-Be-Spoke snarled, interrupting Howie's thoughts. "I need to get on with it. I've been waiting for years to finish what I started when I squished your mommy and daddy. Now it's your turn! Ta-ta, Howie Monroe! One . . . two . . ."

Howie's Writing Journal

Yikes! What am I going to do? I can't let that big obnoxious Evil-Force-Whose-Nam-C'not . . . oh, the heck with it, <u>Herbert</u>, destroy Howie! It just wouldn't be right. I'd get letters. People would stop reading my books. I'D HAVE TO GO BACK TO BEING NOT FAMOUS!! But how am I going to save him?

I'll ask Uncle Harold. Maybe I should ask Pop,

too. (I should probably let my readers know that "Pop" is what I call Chester, the cat I live with, even if he's not in this story. Then again, I could just tell them to see Book 1: <u>It Came from Beneath the Bed!</u> by Howie Monroe and Book 2: <u>Invasion of the Mind Swappers from Asteroid 6!</u>™ by Howie Monroe.)

Okay, I asked Uncle Harold and Pop. Uncle Harold said, "You could try bringing in another character."

Why would I do that? Anyway, I want Howie to save the day, not somebody else.

He also said, "Look carefully at what

you've already written. Maybe the answer is right in front of you."

That means having to go back and actu- ally <u>read</u> what I wrote. Doesn't he know I have better things to do with my time?

Pop was no better. His advice had some- thing to do with getting a life.

Hm, maybe I should do what Uncle Harold suggested. Let's see what happens if I bring another character in unexpectedly.

"I don't have time for so much thinking!" The-Evil-Force-Whose-Nam-C'not-Be-Spoke snarled, interrupting Howie's thoughts. "I need to get on with it. I've been waiting for years to finish what I started when I squished your mommy and daddy. Now it's your turn! Ta-ta, Howie Monroe! One . . . two . . ."

"Stop!" a new voice cried out.

Howie looked around to see who was there. He waited patiently for the author to figure it out.

Suddenly, Hoppy hopped into view! Well, barely into view. Remember, there wasn't much light.

"Hoppy!" Howie said. "What are you doing here?"

"Hoppy is here to help you, sir, and to provide a plot twist at a crucial moment."

CHAPTER 8: "THE TERRIFYING TRANSFORMATION"

"But, Hoppy," said Howie, the thoughtful and considerate, even when his own life was in danger, dachshund, "you could be hurt! You could even be—"

"Transformed into a toaster oven!" bellowed The-Evil-Force-Whose-Nam-C'not-Be-Spoke. There was a blinding flash of light, a deafening roar of thunder, a suffocating puff

of smoke (fortunately, Howie was spared the slide show), and Hoppy was turned into a toaster oven!

"How could you!" Howie cried out in alarm to The-Evil-Force-Whose-Nam-C'not-Be-Spoke. "A toaster oven? You could have turned him into a microwave, at least!"

"Is that what *you'd* like to be? Fine. Get ready to bake potatoes in just ten minutes!"

There was a blinding flash of light, a deafening . . . oh, you get the picture.

Howie squeezed his eyes shut, ready to spend the rest of his life as a kitchen appliance . . . and then it hit him! Not the spell that would turn him into a microwave, but the single word that would break The-Evil-Force-Whose-Nam-C'not-Be-Spoke of his magic.

"No!" Howie cried out. "Don't do it— *Herbert!*"

Light filled the Doghouse of Doom as The-Evil-Force-Whose-Nam-C'not-Be-Spoke, hearing his true name, screamed an ear-splitting scream. Howie watched in horror as the giant shape on the pod in the center of the Lake of Lost Illusions twisted and turned, finally exploding in a shower of sparks.

Howie was forced to close his eyes. When he opened them again, he couldn't believe what he saw!

There, sitting on the pod thing, was a kitten.

"Why, you're nothing but a pussycat," said Howie.

"Yes," said The-Evil-Force-Whose-Nam-Used-To-Be-Not-Able-To-Be-Spoke. "I was once a little pussycat who only wanted love and the occasional saucer of warm milk. But I was left by the side of the road to fend for myself and I turned mean and rotten. So mean and rotten that I picked on others. Your parents didn't understand. They called me a bully. Okay, I was a bully, I admit it. But it was only because I was afraid of being the one who got picked on first."

Wow, Howie thought. *This is even better than watching Oprah.*

Words appeared over Herbert's head. They were written in red smoke. Or . . . was . . . it . . . *ketchup?*

Thank you! ☺

"Gosh," said Howie modestly and graciously, "you're welcome."

"You have given me back my innocence," said Herbert the kitten. "You have given me hope for a new and better life. You have given me—"

"Whatever," said Howie, suddenly remembering Hoppy, the toaster oven. "What about my friend? What are you going to do for *him*?"

"I don't have to do anything," said Herbert. "You've already done that. Look, there in the water!"

"Where are you, Hoppy?" Howie called out.

A tiny voice answered, "Here Hoppy is, sir. Hoppy is happy, sir. Hoppy is where Hoppy always wanted to be, sir."

Howie looked into the water. A happy tadpole was swimming laps.

"Goodbye, Hoppy," Howie said.

"Goodbye, sir," said Hoppy. "Hoppy will always remember you."

"Howie will always remember Hoppy, too," said Howie, sniffing back a tear or two.

Well, Howie thought as he watched Hoppy swim happily away, *I guess I'd better paddle out to the pod and rescue Herbert.*

"I heard that," said the kitten.

CHAPTER 9:
"NOT SAFE YET!"

When Howie emerged from the Doghouse of Doom with Herbert the kitten at his side, everyone cheered. Everyone, that is, but Baco, Grab, and Run, who threw their sign on the ground and stomped on it. Professor Sneak didn't look too pleased, either. Howie decided there was something up about Sneak that would deserve greater attention in another book.

In the meanwhile, he was exhausted. Snivel, Delilah, and several other students carried him on their shoulders to the hospital house, where he spent the next few days sleeping and reading back issues of *Canine Quarterly*. Hamlet visited him regularly and chatted up a storm, sometimes leaving apostrophes lying around on the floor, which had to be swept up after him. Delilah brought up homework assignments from their classes and told him how brave and daring, not to mention courageous, she thought he was. She also asked how his bursitis was. When she did, she fluttered her eyelashes and made his heart go pit-a-pat.

Snivel brought him a box of doggie treats his mother had baked just for the famous, heroic, kind, and wizardly Howie Monroe in the shape of frogs—a nice touch, Howie thought, given how much he missed his friend Hoppy.

Herbert sometimes dropped by to curl up next to him in bed and purr. Over time, Herbert lost his ability to read thoughts, which was a relief to Howie, who had grown tired of hearing Herbert say, "That's what *you* think!"

All in all, Howie was feeling pretty darn good about himself and how he'd handled his first week at the Dogwiz Academy for Canine Conjurers. The fact that he hadn't actually conjured anything yet—except for a quarter, and anybody could do that—didn't worry him. His full powers would come to him in time. He was looking forward to his years at Dogwiz, although not as much as he was looking

forward to his next meal in the Chamber of Chow. A dinner was being planned in his honor, and he could hardly wait.

Back in his own room for the first time in days, he was getting ready to go down to the dinner when a note was slipped under his door. Herbert batted it to him.

It was written in letters that had been cut from what appeared to be issues of *Preteen Conjurer*. It read:

JUST YOU WAIT, MONROE!
YOU'RE NOT SAFE YET!

"This is terrible!" Howie exclaimed.

"No, it's not," said Herbert. "It will give you material for the sequel."

"You're right, Herbert," said Howie. "Thank you."

"It's nothing," said Herbert modestly.

As the two friends went off to join Delilah and Snivel on their way to the Chamber of Chow, Howie was already thinking about his next adventure at the Dogwiz Academy for Canine Conjurers—

Howie Monroe and the Enchanted Chew Bone

THE END?

HOWIE'S WRITING JOURNAL

Delilah read my story and said, "You call that writing? You stole your idea from that book you told me Toby's been reading to you!"

I think she's just sore because she has such a small part in the story.

I asked Uncle Harold what he thought.

"Oh, <u>that's</u> why it all seemed so familiar!" he said. "I don't know, Howie, you might want to be sure it's okay with your editor to—"

"Steal?" I said.

"Ask your editor," he told me.

Great. Now I'm a thief!

Dear Editor:

Here is the manuscript of my latest book. I hope you like it and don't think I'm stealing. If you don't like it or if you *do* think I'm stealing, please don't tell me, because it will mean you won't publish my book and then I will have to go back to not being famous.

Sincerely yours,
Howie Monroe

Dear Howie Monroe:

    I love your new book and
can't wait to publish it. It is
a terrific parody.

                    Yours truly,
                    The Editor

Howie's Writing Journal

par-o-dy/n: writing in which the language and style of an author or work is imitated for comic effect

Comic effect?! This is a serious work of fiction!!!! I can't believe my editor would call it a <u>parody</u>!

I asked Uncle Harold if I should let the editor publish my book if he doesn't even recognize it for what it is!

"Do you want to go back to not being

famous?" Uncle Harold asked me.

Good point.

"Another way to look at it," he went on, "is that you were inspired by some-one else's writing to create something original. Maybe your readers will be inspired by you."

Wow. That would be so cool. Hey, maybe my readers will write <u>Howie Monroe and the Enchanted Chew Bone</u>! Then I wouldn't have to. Not that I don't want to, but, I don't know, I might want to try something really different next time.

Meanwhile, I think it's time for me to take a nap. I've been up for way more than two hours — almost <u>three</u> — and I'm beat! This writing is hard work!